ENIGMA

Enigma

by

Paul T Kidd

Cheshire Henbury

Published in 2014:
Paperback: ISBN 978-1-901864-20-5
Ebook: ISBN 978-1-901864-21-2

British Library Cataloguing in Publication Data.
A catalogue record for this book is available from the British Library.

Cheshire Henbury
Email: books@cheshirehenbury.com

Web site: www.cheshirehenbury.com/enigma

To Marcela and Giuliana for the times that were and the times that are yet to be.

PREFACE

Enigma is an allegorical tale that is related to an earlier book with the title *A Tale of Two Deserts*. This latter book can be described as one book, two tales, one story; and with the addition of *Enigma*, it can be said that now there are two books, many tales and one story. And both books are highly enigmatic.

At the core of *Enigma* is a rather strange and (perhaps to some) crazy story. I leave you, the reader, to interpret the tale and to discover the hidden messages and the lessons that it seeks to impart. As for the narrative that runs across *A Tale of Two Deserts* and *Enigma*, this I also leave for you to discover. And if you struggle to see, to understand, then this also is a lesson as well, for life is a journey of discovery and adventure. This is *Enigma* …

Paul T Kidd
April 2014

"Optimism is a mania for insisting that all is well when all is by no means well"
Voltaire (*Candide*)

"Men's courses will foreshadow certain ends, to which, if persevered in they must lead ..., but if the courses be departed from the ends will change"
Charles Dickens (*A Christmas Carol*)

"Two roads diverged in a wood and I - I took the one less travelled by, and that has made all the difference"
Robert Frost ("The Road Not Taken")

Enigma

And this is the story that I give, to be taken and seen for that which it tells, which is more than unusual and perhaps also slightly crazy, but being so carries with it a warning and a hope, which also is a hallmark of note – here be more words spoken in silence.

"That they danced – this I am sure of, even now after the passage of many years, which has given me time to reflect and to find within me the rationality that enables that which cannot be explained by science, that which does not fit with what is accepted, that which has no place in the modern world, to be pushed out of mind, out of sight. And yet I have not done so!"

The stranger's outburst was unexpected. Many would immediately have concluded that the man was more than just weird, for what he said sounded like gibberish – the beginnings of some ridiculous fantasy story that would leave the listener in no doubt about the lack of the story-teller's sanity and that he was just another crazy person. But that was not my reaction.

He just spoke these words to me, after hours of silence. We were sitting opposite each other as our train proceeded on its way to its final destination as though it had a single-minded determination to do so, taking the only path possible, bound by the limitations of its design to follow the route laid out for it so many years ago, when the railway pioneers, men of business and engineering, built the rail network far back in the nineteenth century. Here for sure was a rare instance of a path not so easily changed.

Some minds are like this as well, but in such cases there is often no good reason not to modify that which is no more than the manifestation of outdated beliefs and values – the invisible chains that bind people to the rock of the past and continue to do so long after what they hold most dear has ceased to be relevant. And thus people become like Prometheus, as do the societies and civilisations in which they dwell, and because of this there are often dire consequences.

I am stating things that might seem to you, dear reader, irrelevant. I am, you perhaps think, wandering off the subject, but I am a writer, an author, so perhaps I am not! And it was because I am a writer that I was inclined to listen as this peculiar man began speaking to me.

In such encounters lies a great potential for the beginning of a new tale or, at least, material to be stored away in the brain, to be brought out when needed in some future storytelling voyage, which is as much a journey of discovery and adventure for me as the author as it is for the reader. I am, one might say, a journey of discovery and adventure.

I did not tell him who I was. I prefer anonymity, and, strangely, we never exchanged names, for we did not speak, so I did not tell him about my roots, my origins, or how I was not a person who wrote, but was, within the fibre of my being, a writer. There is a difference!

I spoke to him without speaking to him, without uttering a single word. One might say that I communicated in silence for I just looked at him and expressed my desire for him to continue through my posture and facial expressions. He read them well.

And this is the story that I give …

"Still it remains with me, a memory of a most enchanting night, when, as a child of seven, I was drawn into a journey of discovery and adventure that was to lead to …

"Perhaps I should not say. I need to reflect upon this before revealing to you where my journey did lead for I think you may regard me as being one of those who suffer from delusions. Yet, do we not all suffer from such?

"It was as though I had been invited, for it seems now, from the vantage point of hindsight, that I was chosen from among the many to see that which, for most, they will never be allowed to understand. For a brief moment the invisible veil – that which shrouds aspects of our world in mystery – was lifted and I beheld something of great importance. Though why I should have been the subject of this revelation I do not know, but I have a feeling that this is something I will learn through a process of discovery that goes by the name of life's journey."

His body language spoke to me as well. He did not seek to hide that he wanted to talk to me, that he had something that he needed to say. Probably this unspoken story had been sitting there in his mind, on his mind, for such a long time until eventually while sitting on a train in front of a stranger he found the courage to speak, to unburden himself of that which had troubled him for an age. Thus it was to me that he turned, in what was perhaps an act of desperation, but possibly also a moment of eventual reckoning, when we do what we know we must – speak about that which has perplexed the mind for many years past. Maybe it was his destiny, my destiny, that one day we would encounter each other, and then … What will happen, will happen! The Arabs have a word for it – *Maktub*; that which is written, that which is known to God, that which cannot be changed. But there are things known to God that can be changed, that should be changed. So change them!

I continued to listen, my curiosity now raised and wanting to hear more, which he duly obliged in delivering.

And this is the story that I give …

"I was, as I have just mentioned, seven years old. It was Christmas night and the time on the clock face spoke of that particular moment in time when the hour passes from Christmas Eve into Christmas Day – 12 midnight.

"Being also such a night I could not sleep so I lay wide awake, listening, and waiting.

"The day had been just like any other Christmas Eve I could remember – full of excitement and anticipation! Time passed, slipping away into the past, and eventually bedtime arrived.

"Reluctantly I made that journey that it seems no child ever wants to make, to bring a day to an end and to enter our dream world, that place where all becomes possible. But here, I hasten to add and to inform you, what I am about to reveal was no dream.

"More time passed by and then I heard my parents also make their own bedtime journey and soon all was quiet.

"Time kept on moving forwards as it always does. Still I could not sleep. Many times I rose from my bed to peep through the curtains at the winter world that lay beyond, hoping to see! But all that could be seen was that

which was visible on any winter's night, which was the
scene always there regardless of the time of year – spring,
summer, autumn and winter. The differences, for there
are always such, were largely defined by nature, and some-
times a little by the hand of man. But nature now is so
different because of humankind and in ways so signifi-
cant that our future is in doubt!

"I decided to take a peep downstairs, to see what
had happened. Perhaps he had already made his visit.
Only one way to discover if this was so!

"So with dressing gown and slippers on, I quietly
moved from bedroom to lounge where our Christmas tree
lay waiting to help us enjoy the coming Christmas Day.

"What of the sight that awaited me? Here I will tell
you something about this, but only in brief.

"There in the lounge was the Christmas tree, of
course, for I have just mentioned this. It stood in the cor-
ner of the room, close by the window, through which I
could just make out the garden, because now there was a
fine dusting of snow on the ground, which always changes
the darkness, making it less.

"The Christmas tree lights had been left switched
on, which I presumed my parents had done so that what

greeted me on Christmas Day morning would be all the
more magical. Of course, as you know, Christmas trees,
when illuminated with multi-coloured lights, are a thing of
great beauty, being so colourful, leaving a special warm-
ing sensation in our minds, which is, I suppose, one of the
reasons why we have them in our homes – to add some
colour and emotion to that which, in most of the northern
hemisphere, is a rather cold and miserable time of year.

"Also there under the tree, clustered around its base,
were many gifts – mostly my Christmas presents – each
one wrapped in paper covered with seasonal images. I
glanced over to the fireplace, to the hearth, and saw there
that the mince pie and sherry that I had left for Father
Christmas had been consumed. So he had been and I had
not heard anything at all!

"I moved towards the tree and sat down cross-
legged on the floor, staring at the scene before my eyes. I
was excited and pondering whether to begin opening my
presents. But something in my mind seemed to be telling
me not to!

"Now as an adult I realise that the mind is peculiar.
It can at times speak to us in ways that we do not understand, nor, it seems, want to, as if to do so is to admit that

there is more to us, to life, to the universe, than people are willing to acknowledge, especially those who are caught up in the world of science."

I knew immediately what he was referring to. So, probably, do you, dear reader, if you care to reflect on the matter for a moment, for you have seen this many times but perhaps not fully recognised it. What am I referring to? I will in a few words explain.

Have you ever heard a scientist who speaks of using science and reason as a way of understanding the world, as though other sources of knowledge and ways of engaging with life, with the universe, and with our complexity, are somehow inferior and therefore not to be taken seriously, for these other sources of understanding are often just remnants of an irrelevant, pre-modern past, and just matters of superstition? You have, for many scientists in these contemporary times think like this and are often to be seen on television preaching this dogma. Yes, I did say preaching dogma, for when looked at closely, these scientists are naught but priests of a religion that they call science. Both religious priest and scientific priest start their careers with the same statement – "I believe!" Both also, it seems, believe in one truth, one best way, and that there is a full, objective true account of everything and that theirs is the sole truth. How peculiar!

Yet what you will not usually see displayed among the high priests of science is much in the way of deep understanding of the true nature of science itself, nor any explanation of what kind of reason these scientific priests are extolling as the way to their truth, for there are many types of reason, just are there are many truths. There is, you see, some complexity concerning the true nature of science and also concepts such as reason, but what scientific priests do not do, on the whole, is spend time questioning the first principles of scientific processes and their beliefs, for if they were to do so, then they would not have time left to undertake any science. And this is partly the source of what can be called the *science delusion*. Yet there are times when such questioning of first principles is essential if there is to ever be any progress, otherwise people become trapped in the past, bound to the rock of the past, so to speak, by invisible chains that few realise are there.

Now you are probably thinking to yourself, "did I not just read something like this a few paragraphs back?

Why is this being repeated?" Indeed I did refer to this matter not many words ago and I am repeating myself. I will here also observe that, with this rock, also frequently come minds that are closed in on fixed opinions and these views are far too often naught but dogma. And another observation is that the madness of science is most often at its greatest when it comes forth speaking of reason, facts and evidence in the name of bettering humanity.

Science on the one hand helps us while at the same time destroying us; we have not yet acquired the knowledge, the sophistication and the wisdom to achieve the former without the latter. Religion also on the one hand helps us while at the same time destroying us; here too we have not yet acquired the knowledge, the sophistication and the wisdom to achieve the former without the latter.

All religions are true. All religions are one. Science and religion are one.

Yes I am repeating myself, so take due note that I do so. I know I seem to digress, but perhaps what I have just said is relevant to the tale that I am recounting to you. This you can judge for yourself, once the tale is told, when all comes together to make the whole, when you will be able to reflect upon the lesson of the story, for without any doubt there is here in my words not just a lesson but also an important warning.

And this is the story that I give …

"I know science is important, but please understand that to question science is also important, essential in fact, and to question is not to reject but to seek to make better.

"Yet I am wandering away from the details of my tale. Therefore I will continue with my explanation.

"So there I was, a seven-year-old sitting cross-legged on the floor in front of our family Christmas tree, with Christmas gifts, all very enticing, waiting, as though inviting me to open them. And it was just after one o'clock in the morning. Yet I hesitated, which I suppose is what led to the events that I will soon explain, for had my mind become engaged with opening presents and playing with toys, I would not have noticed some quite peculiar happenings! Thus it was that because of this, of focusing on what was occurring, I went on my journey of discovery and adventure."

Life is strange. When he uttered these words I instantly knew that he spoke of something we often do not care to consider. We are all, it seems, living our lives as distracted people, not noticing what is going on around us. We do not examine what is taking place within our own lives, among those close to us, within our environment, so pre-occupied are we with our materialistic existence. Nature dies before us, yet few notice this. But there are also other matters that we do not take time to observe, prefer-ring to ignore such, for what I speak of increasingly has no place in people's lives, for they think themselves, ex-plicitly or tacitly, as nothing more than machines, and not having souls, feel no need to nourish that which they have convinced themselves does not exist. It is now truly a case that – to paraphrase Isaac Newton – people have become like children playing on the seashore, diverting themselves in now and then finding a smoother pebble or a prettier shell than ordinary, while the great ocean of truth lies all undiscovered before them, for they have taken the decision to ignore it. This is what happens when sci-ence goes wrong, when materialism takes hold, when the mind conquers and our delusions are victorious. And we wonder why there is so much madness in the world!

And this is the story that I give …

"I noticed that the tree was trembling slightly, but that nothing else in the room was being disturbed at all. These vibrations grew in magnitude and it was as though the tree was coming alive, more alive, that is, than a tree – being biological in nature, but not in the same way as us – can be said to be alive, even when separated from the roots that provide its nourishment, for even then, although the link be broken, life still continues, but only for a while, just like the soul, for it too lives on when it is denied that which is needed to sustain it; but again, only for a while.

"The tree was not the only aspect of what lay before me that was changing. As the Christmas tree started to spring into life the wall lying immediately behind it began to disappear, and manifesting itself as its replacement was a vista of a snow-covered forest where, in the distance, an illuminated area could be observed, as though within the tree-studded landscape there was some small settlement lit up by its inhabitants to drive away the darkness of the night.

"I suppose you think now that this is a dream, for there can be no other explanation. But I know that what I experienced was no dream for there is something that proves to me that it was not and about this I will explain as my tale comes to an end.

"Our Christmas tree had now become fully animated and began to move away from me, into the forest scene that lay behind it. Yes, indeed, our tree was, in a way, walking, and it was also heading off towards this light that I have only just mentioned. I rose and followed, not of course thinking, for by now I was fully enchanted by what was taking place and felt no fear at all. This was, for me, truly a journey of discovery and adventure and, not being inhibited in the same way that an adult mind would have been, I was full willing to participate in the wonder of the events unfolding before me.

"So, after taking a few short steps I found myself in this snow-covered world, but I was not feeling cold, nor did my slippers become wet with the snow, which I suppose can be attributed to the magic – if one wants to call it such – by which my adventure was enabled.

"It was as though I had stepped through a door and what lay beyond this door was a world of beautiful and astonishing things, and being a child, unencumbered by the delusions of the adult mind, I did not find it hard to gather the courage to do what my soul was telling me to do, to take the first steps, to discover this astounding world. This was truly the beginning of a journey of discovery and adventure, for it was without any doubt a journey of the soul that led me to …

"I am back to this point again and now, having reflected upon the matter while speaking, I think I will reveal something of this to you, but perhaps not all! Not this time, at least! Perhaps more will follow later. Who knows!"

I sensed that the stranger was now coming to the central and most important part of his story and I was by now fully engrossed, waiting with anticipation, for what was before me was evidently a tale in full and one that I knew could be taken, just as it was being given and laid out as a rather original story, as a fable most unusual, one very weird, but nicely so.

The man continued speaking.

And this is the story that I give …

"As I observed and participated in these strange happenings, events became even odder, which, if you have not yet understood, is the hallmark of my tale.

"Following our Christmas tree, which was leading the way, I trudged through the snow past many other trees that stood motionless, for there was no wind or life-animating force to make this not so.

"I do not know how far or for how long we walked, always the tree leading and myself following, but what I can say is that we were heading towards that illuminated place that I have already mentioned.

"As I – we – drew closer, the intensity of the light increased and my curiosity was much raised and I suppose, also my childish wonder; I wished to know what it was that glowed so bright in that dark night. It was a surprise to me and I think it will also be one to you.

"Now I will not go on hiding from you what it is that I discovered, for now I have reached the point in my story where we had arrived at what at first I thought was a large clearing in the forest. But it was more than this, for I soon realised I had reached the very edge of the forest and here was the source of the light and beyond it there was darkness.

"The reason for the darkness will very soon be explained, but first I will tell you about the source of the light.

"My Christmas tree was not alone! Here, gathered at the edge of the forest, were thousands upon thousands of Christmas trees, every one lit up with lights, some coloured, some not, but all aglow, be they big lights or very small ones.

"And they were all dancing, as merry as can be, caught up in the moment and oblivious to what was taking place around them.

"They were like children playing on the seashore, diverting themselves in now and then finding a smoother pebble or a prettier shell than ordinary, while the great ocean of truth lay all undiscovered before them, for they too, it seemed, had taken the decision to ignore it.

"But it was no seashore that they played on! They were blind to something that they should have taken note of.

"I stood with my Christmas tree, at the edge of the forest, watching the dancing trees. Then my tree began to move forward once more, into the melee of dancing trees, and I followed, with those highly animated trees moving apart as we approached, creating for us a path through the crowd.

"And the noise that emanated from this moving forest of brightly coloured trees! Oh, what noise they made – a cacophony of jingling bells, of baubles banging against one another, of rustling branches, of crunching of snow. It was deafening!

"Through this we passed until at last we approached the centre where I observed what seemed to be an old man, yet about this I was not too certain. Old he most definitely was. But as for being a man, this I am not sure about! He was also simultaneously both familiar and unfamiliar. And this Being was seated and seemed agitated, as if it was trying to calm the frenzy, but with little effect.

"As I approached, as I drew closer, my presence was noticed, and I think there was some gladness that I was there. Through gestures I was encouraged to move closer, which I did, until I was standing close enough to see into this strange Being's eyes, where I thought I saw concern writ large.

"Then words were spoken to me, but I could not make out anything meaningful in what was said, such was the noise and the distraction around me. As hard as the Being tried, communication with me was virtually impossible and all I could discern were a few words, scattered here and there, which made whatever it was that the Being said something of a confused message.

"While speaking, this rather odd Being often looked towards the darkness that I have already mentioned, gesturing to me, asking me, I thought, to do something, but I did not know what. I tried to ask what it was that was wanted of me, but the reply was once more lost in the sounds that engulfed us, so I did not see that what was being told to me was a warning about that which was about to happen.

"If only I had realised. If only I had understood. Then perhaps what was soon to occur could have been avoided. I will never know."

At this moment the stranger placed his hand into his pocket and produced something the likes of which I had never seen before. It was a stone, but no ordinary piece of rock, for it was red as a ruby, a precious gem for sure; but this was no small cut stone that one sees in a brooch or other items of jewellery.

I will tell you that it was big, about the size of a large egg, and it was not entirely red for within it were specks of blue, as if sapphires had somehow become trapped within the rock when it had formed. But mysteriously the blue parts glowed, which created a strange visual effect. It was indeed an object of great beauty as well as mystery, for not only was it unusual but, I would say, unearthly in origin as well.

I felt a desire to touch it and so I reached out to take hold of the stone, but the stranger quickly pulled back his hand, indicating also through his body language that he was not prepared to let the precious object leave his possession, even for a few brief seconds, at least not at that moment.

I understood and acknowledged this by leaning back into my seat, for by now I had drawn closer to the man and was bent forward, arms folded and resting on the table that separated us.

He slipped the unusual object back into his pocket and continued with his monologue.

And this is the story that I give ...

"Did I not say that I had something that proved that what happened that night was no dream? Have you ever seen a rock like that? I think you have not!

"I was given what you have just seen by this Being who sat at the centre of events, but not at the point in my tale that I have now reached. This came later, after … When it was over, when the disaster that befell the dancing trees …

"If only I had understood what was being communicated to me. If only I had known what that darkness represented and what lay beyond that place where we stood. Perhaps I could have prevented the events that were soon to transpire.

"But I did not and history became what it now is. This I feel sure, though, was a history that was not meant to be. My story could have been a different one, but it is not and now there is nothing I can do about it, other than telling my tale to you.

"I should, I think, now tell what remains and draw this rather unusual account of a childhood adventure to a close.

"Thus, while standing there trying hard to understand what the Being was saying to me, the mood of the party, if indeed that is what it was, began to change. The trees, the dancing trees, they seemed to dance even more intensely as though encouraged by some invisible force and they were also growing more confident.

"I remained where I stood, with the Being that had tried to speak to me, along with my Christmas tree, which fortunately was not dancing.

"The Being's demeanour had now changed. It looked sad and disappointed and I wondered why for I could not see any cause for this, at least not at that moment in time, but this reason was about to become clear.

"Slowly I became aware that there seemed to be fewer trees than there had been a few minutes previously. Perhaps not, though, for the mind is indeed a strange thing. So I tried to dismiss this thought from my mind, but it would not go away.

"I continued to watch until there was no doubt that the number of dancing trees had diminished.

"My assumption at this moment was that trees were beginning to depart, which was not entirely incorrect. Hence, on thinking this, I ventured towards the darkness and in doing so I found myself following the remaining Christmas trees, which were now few in number until …

"I stopped. Then I watched as those trees ahead of me just disappeared. The party, the dancing trees, these were no more. All that was left was the Being, my own Christmas tree and me. Now I understood what the Being had been trying to say.

"I had been given a warning and asked to do something to stop the trees from wandering too close to the edge of a precipice, for this is what they were doing. And the result of my inaction was that every single one of them had fallen into an abyss. This, you see, was the source of the darkness, for there was no land, just a vast ocean with waves crashing on the shore at the base of the cliffs from which the dancing trees had fallen. And here now they all lay, broken, destroyed, never to dance again. For them, life, their existence, was over.

"I turned away and returned to where the Being was seated. All now was calm and all that I could hear were the sounds of nature, with the noise of waves breaking on a shore not so far away.

"Even now, though, with the din created by the dancing trees no more hindering communications, I was still not able to perceive what the Being was saying to me. Then I began to understand that communicating with this entity was not at all simple, for the language spoken was one that I, being human, could not easily understand.

"And it was at this moment that I was given that most unusual of stones."

The train now was slowing as it was approaching its next stop and the stranger had ceased speaking to glance out of the window. Then he was gone.

I peered out through the glass and watched him disappear among the crowd of people that had disembarked. Then the train was once more on its way, heading towards the final destination, and I was left pondering the peculiar tale that I had just been told, and how, again I note this, we had not shared a word in conversation.

And now you have the story, and can make of it what you will, for this is the story that I give to you.

And here is another story that I give …

Many years have passed, time moving onwards, taking me with it, and you too, and towards a different destination than the one expected – such is life!

I sit in a room, in a distant city, the city of the stars, thinking about that stranger and his most unusual of tales. I am wondering what to do about it and thinking also about its meaning.

In my mind's eye I see children playing at the edge of a cliff, and they, being children, are not mindful of the dangers, so they wander too close to the edge. How often, I wonder, do they do this? Perhaps too often! Yet still they play. And still they are watched, cared for, protected, lest they fall and all should end.

This is the unwritten, untold story, and one that begins in a distant past that lies beyond recorded history, but of which there are remnants left, being bound up in other tales, which, protected by taboos, have been passed down from generation to generation, across the ages of man. And within these preserved and largely unchanging stories, here and there you might see, if you know how to look, and what to seek, tales of dancing trees.

I am wondering what to do, for I know I must act. But how? This is a question that I had not before considered, for in finding, in discovering, it did not occur to me, at least at the start, how I would broach this subject. But I did not need to, for events did this for me, which led me to a giving of words, for it was no conversation as such.

And the giving of words is what this story is about, and also the other one that I have recounted above for you, and others too. Note them well.

My right hand is inside my jacket pocket, my left, resting on the table. I speak, she listens. She probably thinks I am a crazy person. By the benchmark of the human mind, with its love of the rational, I am most definitely crazy and this, as I have already told you, is a hallmark of note, for what I speak of is not for the mind, but for the soul, and that is different from the mind, and what is spoken of here most definitely is the language of the soul. Judge it not therefore by the standards set by the mind.

I speak some more and in doing so I recount yet another story. I say that it is as though I am, every day, journeying out from an oasis, searching for a new path, and each day I go a little further, but always come back. I speak of a day coming when returning will look less attractive than just travelling onwards, and so when that day comes I will just keep on moving. Such a day is approaching. One day I will not be able to come back, for I will be no more. And yet also I will still be.

The quest to find a different trail, a new path, is a lifelong one that begins many times across a lifetime.

I speak of a voice, not real, but figurative, and this voice that is not a voice grows louder and clearer. Now I know she is wondering, thinking, who is this crazy person! Yet she still listens for the soul speaks a different language to the mind.

What I am about to give her might be seen as a key to a door, but some doors cannot be opened for you – only the person holding the key can do that. And beyond this door, what lies there?

If you want to know in detail you must open it, but, as a hint, what can be found beyond the door are the beginnings of answers, reasons, causes of that which perplexes the mind – the mind, you see, will always have some things shut out. It wants to know, but when you speak the truth that comes from the soul, soon it is saying, "What nonsense is this? I do not want to hear anymore. Be quiet for you disturb me too much."

And I can tell you, for it is always so, that you will be surprised by what lies beyond this door – a world of beautiful and astonishing things. So I ask a question: can you find the courage to do what your soul is telling you to do, to take the first steps, to discover this astounding world, to follow the path that is yours to take?

If you do, I can promise you that what you encounter will truly be a journey of discovery and adventure, for it will be a journey of the soul that will lead you to …

My right hand is still in my jacket pocket. I take hold of what lies there and, taking it from its place of rest, carefully position it on the table in front of her and in doing so pass it on. It is a symbolic act, this giving, this passing-on of that which was given to me, a long time ago and in the strangest of circumstances.

So the stone, if that is what it is, being the size of a large egg, just sits there on the table in front of her. And it is ruby red, but not entirely so, for within there are specks of blue, as if sapphires had somehow become trapped within the rock when it had formed. Mysteriously, these blue parts glow, which creates a strange visual effect. It is indeed an object of great beauty as well as mystery, for not only is it unusual but, I would say, unearthly in origin as well.

And now you have another story, and you can make of it what you will, for this too is the story that I give to you.

And here is a further story that I give …

The trees, they danced, caught up with the wind, and all life was there to behold. Shaking, stirring, they were lost in their minds and not at all taking note. The dance continued, a frenzy of joy, and thus the greater their determination, the more they danced. And the universe, it speaks of things that will be, of what must not be, and of that which should be. These are messages, timeless, eternal, enduring, but few are able to hear, to see, to understand. With messages written in the stars, and words carried on the wind, you must learn to read. So now quieten that deafening noise, calm that troubled mind, open those unseeing eyes, and then listen to that silent voice.

Once they danced, the trees, they danced, but now they dance no more. It does not have to be so.

And now you have a further story, and can make of it what you will, for this too is the story that I give to you.

And here is yet one more story that I give …

And then there was the earth, where other life once more flourished, for time healed the scars and nature was reborn, and it was as though man had never been, because nature reclaimed that which had been taken, transforming it all back into fine grains of dust, for what had been no more than dust was once more that which it had been. This is a future that could be, but does not have to be.

And now you have one more story and can make of it what you will, for this too is the story that I give to you.

And here is the story that I give …

Life is like a garden where souls are the plants and the soil is the body; both need to be nurtured, protected, and tended well.

And now you have the story, and can make of it what you will, for this is the story that I give to you.

And here is the story that I give …

When people consume the fruit of the tree of knowledge and do not also feed the soul, they shall surely perish.

And now you have the story, and can make of it what you will, for this is the story that I give to you.

And here is the story that I give …

The books, the stories, and the writings are one, being as they are all written by the same hand.

And now you have the story, and can make of it what you will, for this is the story that I give to you.

And here is the story that I give ...

All human life is sacred and the taking of a human life is wrong; there are no exceptions.

And now you have the story, and can make of it what you will, for this is the story that I give to you.

And here is the story that I give ...

Nature too is sacred so live not like a locust, but be instead a lotus.

And now you have the story, and can make of it what you will, for this is the story that I give to you.

And here is the story that I give ...

There are many truths and no one has discovered these truths.

And now you have the story, and can make of it what you will, for this is the story that I give to you.

And here is the story that I give …

You will never be alone; one life lived as two.

And now you have the story, and can make of it what you will, for this is the story that I give to you.

And here is the story that I give …

Be the gardener that you were born to be.

And now you have the story, and can make of it what you will, for this is the story that I give to you.

And here is the story that I give …

See it out to the edge of doom.

And now you have the story, and can make of it what you will, for this is the story that I give to you.

And here is the story that I give …

Come to know me on your own.

And now you have the story, and can make of it what you will, for this is the story that I give to you.

And here is the story that I give …

Enigma …